TREASURE AHOY!

Pirates Can Share

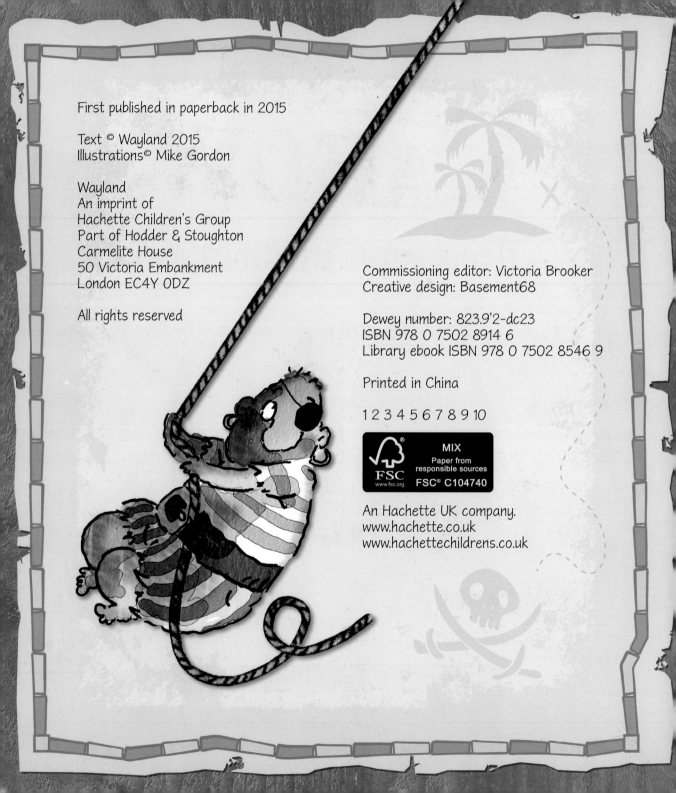

First published in paperback in 2015

Text © Wayland 2015
Illustrations© Mike Gordon

Wayland
An imprint of
Hachette Children's Group
Part of Hodder & Stoughton
Carmelite House
50 Victoria Embankment
London EC4Y 0DZ

Commissioning editor: Victoria Brooker
Creative design: Basement68

Dewey number: 823.9'2-dc23
ISBN 978 0 7502 8914 6
Library ebook ISBN 978 0 7502 8546 9

Printed in China

1 2 3 4 5 6 7 8 9 10

MIX
Paper from
responsible sources
FSC
www.fsc.org
FSC® C104740

An Hachette UK company.
www.hachette.co.uk
www.hachettechildrens.co.uk

TREASURE AHOY!

Pirates Can Share

Written by
Tom Easton

Illustrated by
Mike Gordon

WAYLAND

Some people say bad luck comes
in threes. It certainly seemed that way one
stormy night on board the *Golden Duck*.

Firstly, Captain Cod
fell down some stairs
and broke his wooden leg.

Secondly, Nell fell overboard!

The other pirates pulled her out,
but she'd lost her favourite bandanna,
the only one without a hole.

Thirdly, and perhaps worst of all, poor Polly Parrot was hit by a bolt of lightning as the storm raged. She lost most of her feathers.

The next day, the battered ship stopped
at an island to make some repairs.

"Go ashore and see if you can find some oak wood I can use for a new leg," the Captain ordered Sam.

"And try and find a parrot willing to sell some of his feathers to Polly," Davy Jones called. Polly squawked in agreement.

"And keep your eye
out for a new bandanna,"
Nell added. They all looked at her.
Nell shrugged. "There might be shops."

Sam trudged around the island,
twice. There were no oak trees, no parrots
and certainly no shops. He sighed and turned
to head back to the ship when he tripped
on something half-buried in the sand.

It was a bag of gold coins!

Sam tucked the bag into his
pocket and returned to the ship.

"Sorry everyone. I didn't find anything," he lied. Everyone looked very glum.

That night, Sam tossed and turned
in his mouldy old hammock.

He kept thinking of all the things he
could buy with his gold coins.

A few days later the *Golden Duck* arrived at a bustling harbour.

The pirates talked
about going ashore.

"I think I'll stay here," the Captain said, sadly. "I can't walk very well without my leg."

"I'll stay with you," Nell said kindly.

"Don't you want to look at the shops?" Sam asked her.
"I can't afford a new bandanna anyway," she said, shaking her head.

Sam wandered through the harbour town.
He passed a sweet shop,

a cutlass shop...

...and a hammock shop.

Where should he
spend his money?

Sam returned to the ship that night with a large sack and a big grin. "What's in the sack?" Davy Jones asked.

Sam reached in and pulled out a brand new bandanna with no holes, just lots of polka dots.

He gave it to Nell.
"Thanks, Sam!" she
grinned and gave
him a pirate kiss.

Next, Sam took out
a handful of feathers.
Polly squawked in
delight and ran off
to stick them on.

"Anything else in there?"
the Captain asked hopefully.
Sam winked and pulled
out a new wooden leg.
"It's beautiful," the Captain
said, his eyes wide. "But where
did you get the money?"

Sam told the pirates about his lucky find on the island. "Sharing with us was very generous," Davy Jones said. "It was the right thing to do," Sam agreed.

"Oh, and I nearly forgot," Sam said.
"I visited one more shop today."
He reached into the sack
and brought out...

NOTES FOR PARENTS AND TEACHERS

Pirates to the Rescue

The books in the 'Pirates to the Rescue' series are designed to help children recognise the virtues of generosity, honesty, politeness and kindness.
Reading these books will show children that their actions and behaviour have a real effect on people around them, helping them to recognise what is right and wrong, and to think about what to do when faced with difficult choices.

Treasure Ahoy!

'Treasure Ahoy' is intended to be an engaging and enjoyable read for children aged 4-7. The book will help children recognise why it's right to share and also that being generous is its own reward.
Sharing is an important skill for children to learn and also one of the hardest. Sharing a room with a sibling, sharing toys with schoolmates, sharing a treat with a friend, these can all difficult for children to accept. But these are also rewarding behaviours, something children can understand with guidance and reassurance.

Learning to share helps children to develop relationships with others, to learn how their behaviour affects others and to understand each other's feelings. Some children find it difficult to think about others. Sharing is a vital skill in developing consideration for others, an essential part of growing up. To have another child share with you is useful for developing self-esteem and learning to express gratitude and develop friendships.

Suggested follow-up activities

When Sam finds the gold coins, his first thought is to keep them for himself. Ask your child whether he or she would do the same. What would your child spend the money on? When Sam is lying in his hammock, he begins to have second thoughts. Discuss with your child why Sam might be having such doubts. What are his feelings?

Ask your child to put him or herself in the position of the captain, Nell or Polly when they can't go ashore. How do they feel? Why does Nell decide not to go ashore? How does Sam feel when he sees his friends are sad?

When Sam is in the town, deciding what shop to go in, ask your child again what they would spend the money on. Discuss the options. When Sam returns to the ship with gifts for his friends, ask your child how this made the captain, Nell and Polly feel. Most importantly, how does sharing his wealth with his friends make Sam feel?

Children could be encouraged to relate an example of a time when they shared something, or a time when they didn't. How did sharing/not sharing make them feel? Has your child felt injustice when a friend or sibling would not share? Explain that others will feel the same way if your child won't share in turn.

Take care to share with your child yourself. Prepare a plate of a favourite treat and ask your child if he or she will share it with you. Say 'Here's one for you. Here's one for me. We're sharing!' Or during play time, share toys. 'You play with this doll, I'll play with that one. We're sharing.' Then arrange to swap the toys.

Don't forget to share things with your partner, or older siblings. Make a show of it. Young children watch and imitate adult behaviour. Recognise and praise sharing whenever you see it. 'I liked the way you gave your sister one of your sweets. Well done.' A reward chart may be a good way to keep track of achievements. Add a star every time your child makes an effort to share.

Ask your child to draw a picture of the pirates in this book and then to draw something they'd like to share with them.

BOOKS TO SHARE

Don't Play Dirty, Gertie: Play Fair (You Choose)
by Lisa Regan (Wayland, 2012)

The 'You Choose' series explores dilemmas that all children face.
Amusing and simple multiple choice questions encourage children to look
at different ways to resolve situations and decide which choice they would
make, while helping the character in the book choose the RIGHT thing to do.

Not Fair, Won't Share (Our Emotions)
by Sue Graves (Watts, 2011)

Miss Clover has made a space station. Posy, Ben and Alfie must take turns
to play with it. But Posy doesn't want to share, and everyone gets cross.
Can the children learn to enjoy it together?

Rainbow Fish
by Mark Pfister (North-South Books, 2007)

An award-winning book about a beautiful fish who finds friendship
and happiness when he learns to share.

Sharing a Shell
by Julia Donaldson (Macmillan, 2005)

The tiny hermit crab loves his new shell. He doesn't want to share
it — not with a blobby purple anenome and a tickly bristleworm.
But life in the rock pool proves tougher than Crab thinks,
and soon he finds he needs his new housemates in this lovely
story of sea, shells and friendship.